For all the little wolves who, despite their belief,
are so beautiful.

Orianne Lallemand

The Wolf
Who Wanted to Change His Color

Text by Orianne Lallemand
Illustrations by Eleonore Thuillier

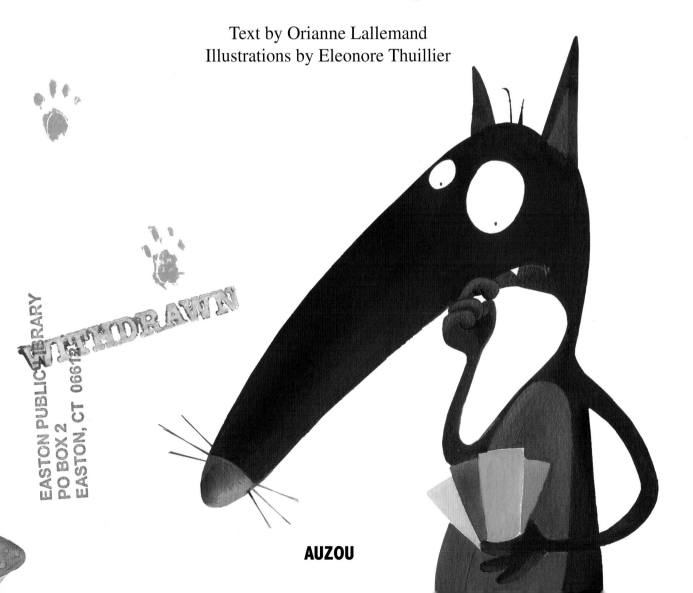

AUZOU

Once upon a time, there was a big,
gray wolf that did not like his color.
He thought that **gray** was much too dreary.

But Wolf had an idea:
he would change his color!

Monday

On Monday, the wolf tried **green**.
He plunged his paw into a tin
of green paint and smeared
the paint all over his body.

When the paint dried, the wolf looked at himself in the mirror.
"What an awful sight!" he exclaimed.
"Now I look like a fat frog. This will not do at all!"

Tuesday

On Tuesday, the wolf slipped on his **red** sweater, which his grandmother had knitted for him, and a pair of scarlet stockings.

When he had on his red clothes, the wolf looked at himself in the mirror. "Goodness me! Now I look like Santa Claus. And I don't even like Christmas! No, this will not do at all!"

On Wednesday, the wolf snuck into the farmer's garden and picked all the pink roses.

Wednesday

Then he covered himself
in the pink petals.

When he was covered in **pink**,
he looked at himself in the mirror.

"Yuck!" he shrieked.
"Now I look like a princess.
No, this will not do at all!"

Thursday

On Thursday, the wolf plunged himself into an ice-cold bath.

He was so cold, that when he came out of the bath, he had turned blue.
As his teeth chattered, he looked at himself in the mirror.
"Brrr! B-b-blue makes m-m-me look hideous. N-no, th-this will n-not do at all!"

On Friday, the wolf ate an entire basket full of oranges.
Then he carefully stuck the orange peels all over his body.

Friday

When he finished, he looked at himself in the mirror.

"How dreadful!" he exclaimed.

"I look like a giant carrot, and maybe even like a wolf. No, this will not do at all!"

Saturday

On Saturday, the wolf rolled around in a big puddle of mud.

When he was all **brown**,
he looked at himself in the mirror.

"Goodness me!
Now I don't look like anything
at all. Besides, the mud makes
me itch, and I smell awful.
No, this will not do at all!"

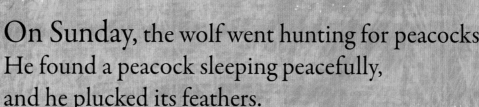

Sunday

On Sunday, the wolf went hunting for peacocks.
He found a peacock sleeping peacefully,
and he plucked its feathers.

After he dressed in his peacock feathers,
he looked at himself in the mirror.

"Ooh! This time,
I do look handsome!"

But all the female wolves thought
he looked handsome too!
All day long, they followed him
around and whispered into his ear,
"Oh, how handsome you are,
my dear wolf!"

The poor **multicolored** wolf
had no peace at all.

Finally, one evening, when he could stand it no more,
the wolf looked at himself in the mirror.

"This won't do at all!
I don't want to be **green**,
red, **pink**, **blue**, **orange**,
brown, or even **multicolored!**'

"Finally, I am happy being just the way I am ...
a **gray** wolf!"

General Director: Gauthier Auzou
Senior Editor: Florence Pierron
English Version Editor: Nelson Yomtov
Layout: Annaïs Tassone
Translation from French: Susan Allen Maurin
Original title: *Le loup qui voulait changer de couleur*
© Éditions Auzou, Paris (France), 2011
(English version)
ISBN: 978-2-7338-1945-6

Printed and bound in China, November 2011.

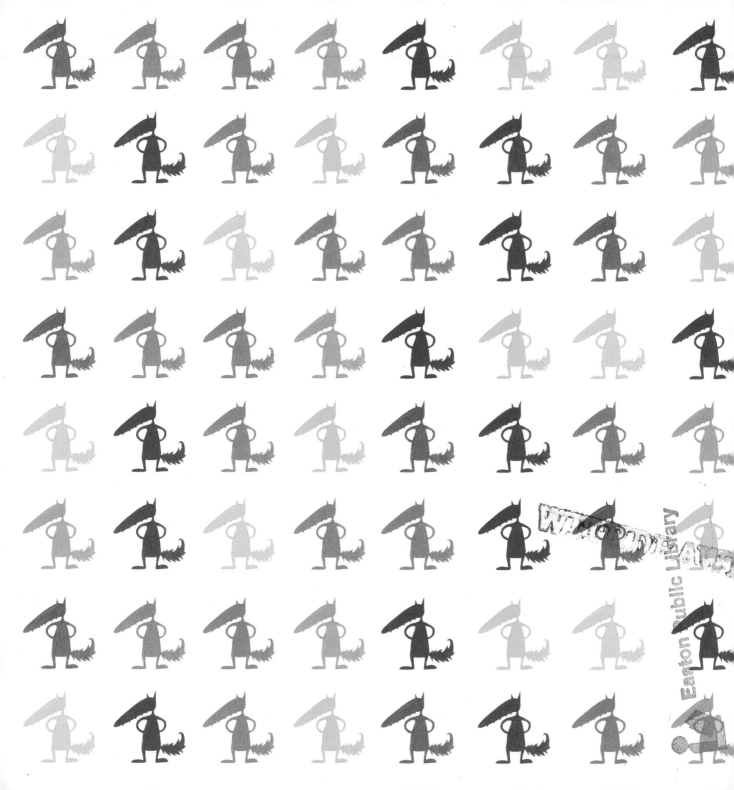